To Pete, Caitlin,

    and the Mighty Huffer

Copyright © 1999 by Bob Graham

First U.S. edition 1999

Library of Congress Cataloging-in-Publication Data

Graham, Bob, date.
Benny : an adventure story / Bob Graham.—1st U.S. ed.
p.   cm.
Summary: When Benny the dog steals the show
from Brillo the magician, he is forced to look for a new home
where his rare talents such as juggling and tap dancing
will be appreciated.
ISBN 0-7636-0813-0
[1. Dogs—Fiction. 2. Magicians—Fiction.]   I. Title
PZ7.G751667Be   1999
[E]—dc21   98-29210

10 9 8 7 6 5 4 3 2 1

Printed in Hong Kong

This book was typeset in Garamond Book Educational.
The pictures were done in watercolor and ink.

Candlewick Press
2067 Massachusetts Avenue
Cambridge, Massachusetts 02140

Benny

An Adventure Story

Bob Graham

CANDLEWICK PRESS

CAMBRIDGE, MASSACHUSETTS

Benny had skills that were rare in a dog. As an assistant to Brillo the Magician, he did his job well enough . . . But Benny had talents all of his own. He could juggle three clubs at once and throw a rope like a cowboy.

He could escape from the
Houdini Deathtrap while
playing the harmonica.
"Bravo!" cried the audience.

His tap dancing met with thunderous applause,
and how the dust rose from those well-trodden boards!

Brillo muttered darkly under his moustache.

Benny was becoming more popular than he was.

"OUT! and never come back!" cried Brillo.

Benny's bottom lip quivered with emotion
as he left the stage forever.

He spent his last coins on a can of dog food and a can opener.

In a bleak railroad yard he ate

the last of his lamb chunks and pasta.

He wiped his mouth on his spotted scarf, and then . . .

Benny jumped aboard
a moving freight train.

To the rhythm of the wheels,
he tapped his foot and sang,
"Oh, *blue is me!*
Oh, dearie me,
I'm as down as
a dog can be."

And while he slept, the train
continued its rhythm:
OUT, OUT . . .
and never come back.
OUT, OUT . . .
and never come back.

Benny woke the next morning
to the smell of fresh-cut grass
and countryside.

He put his harmonica in his
bag and leapt off the train.
"I will bring my tricks
to the world," he said.

But the world did not want Benny's tricks. Nobody wanted a dancing sheepdog.

Nobody wanted a tiny rope-throwing cattle dog.

Nobody wanted a plate-juggling kitchen dog.

Nobody wanted
a guard dog
who played
the harmonica.

Only one person
wanted a wanderer
like Benny . . .

but Benny did
not want HIM!

"I will find myself a home,"
he said and set off in search of one.

He sat above the roaring engines of mighty road trucks.

He crossed rivers

and deserts.

He stood on
mountains and
moaned at
the moon.

Then one day Benny stopped. He put down his bag,
wiped his brow, and looked around him.

"I can go no farther," he said.

"I'm not a sheepdog, a cattle dog, a kitchen dog
or a guard dog. So what sort of dog am I?"

"I am Benny!
And I will do
what I do.
And this time,
the world shall
come to me."

Benny's feet beat out the rhythm of the train on the tracks,
and his harmonica howled like the desert wind and
pulsed like the engines of the mighty road trucks.

Many coins rattled into Benny's cup that day, and many faces passed by. Then someone stood in front of him. His breath stopped. His feet stopped. The sun came out.

It was Mary Kelly.

And Mary's mother,   and her father,   and her brother,

and her grandma,   and her grandad,

and her baby sister,
Morag.

For Benny, and the Kellys too,
it was love at first sight.
Off he went, the coins heavy in his cup.
At last, he had found a place to call home.

Now, each night after
dinner, the music starts,
and each night the
floorboards shake.
Mary's and Benny's feet
beat to the rhythm of
the jigs and the reels.

And Benny lives up there,
on the hill, to this day.